# Shape Up . . . or Else!

"Well, did you find the troublemaker yet?" Brenda asked in a hurried voice.

"Not yet," Nancy said. "But I think I'm getting close."

"Not good enough," Brenda snapped. "A photographer from *Today's Times* is coming to school tomorrow. Nothing can go wrong!"

"I said I was close," Nancy said. "And I'm working as hard as I can."

"Well, work harder," Brenda said. "Because if Alice writes a crummy article about our school, it will be *your* fault."

## The Nancy Drew Notebooks

Available from MINSTREL Books

# THE
# NANCY DREW
# NOTEBOOKS®

#35

*Third-Grade Reporter*

## CAROLYN KEENE
ILLUSTRATED BY JAN NAIMO JONES

A MINSTREL® BOOK

Published by POCKET BOOKS
New York   London   Toronto   Sydney   Singapore

This book is a work of fiction. Names, characters, places and incidents are products of the author's imagination or are used fictitiously. Any resemblance to actual events or locales or persons living or dead is entirely coincidental.

A MINSTREL PAPERBACK *Original*

 A Minstrel Book published by
POCKET BOOKS, a division of Simon & Schuster Inc.
1230 Avenue of the Americas, New York, NY 10020

Copyright © 2000 by Simon & Schuster Inc.

ISBN: 0-671-04266-1

First Minstrel Books printing April 2000

10  9  8  7  6  5  4  3  2  1

NANCY DREW, THE NANCY DREW NOTEBOOKS, A MINSTREL BOOK and colophon are registered trademarks of Simon & Schuster Inc.

Cover art by Joanie Schwarz

Printed in the U.S.A.

PHX/✶

# 1

# Welcome, Miss Snobby Pants

**W**hy would a grown-up want to come back to elementary school?" Nancy Drew's best friend George Fayne asked.

Nancy smiled at the sign on the school door. It read, Welcome Back, Alice Stone. Underneath was Alice's old third-grade school picture.

"Alice isn't just any grown-up, George," Nancy said. "She's a reporter for *Today's Times*, and she's writing a whole article about our school."

Nancy was so excited she had hardly slept the night before. Alice Stone would be in Mrs. Reynolds's class from Monday to Thursday. On Friday she would go back to *Today's Times* to write her article.

"Do you think Mrs. Reynolds will give Alice homework?" Bess Marvin asked. Bess was Nancy's other best friend. She was also George's cousin.

"Sure," Nancy said. "Alice is going to be one of us for almost a whole week."

"That is going to be so cool!" George said, her dark eyes flashing.

"Excuse me," a voice behind Nancy said. "You can thank *me* for that!"

Nancy rolled her eyes. She would know that voice anywhere—it belonged to snooty Brenda Carlton. Brenda's father owned *Today's Times*. Brenda even had her own newspaper, which she wrote at home on her computer. It was called the *Carlton News*.

"Did I tell you that it was *my* idea to invite Alice to our school?" Brenda asked as the girls turned around.

"A million times!" George groaned.

Brenda flipped her brown hair over one shoulder. "One day while I was visiting my father's newspaper—"

"Here comes a million and *one*," Bess whispered.

"—I met Alice!" Brenda went on. "When Alice told me she'd gone to Carl Sandburg Elementary School I said she should come back to visit. Guess what Alice said?"

"What?" Nancy asked. But she really knew the answer.

"She said she'd love to!" Brenda declared. "Alice also said she'd write a whole article about being back at her old school."

"Then it was Alice's idea, not yours." Bess said.

Brenda glared at Bess. "It was *so* my idea, Bess Marvin!" she snapped.

Bess shook her head. "*Nuh*-uh."

"Uh-*huh!*" Brenda exclaimed.

"It doesn't matter whose idea it was," Nancy said. "What's important is that we're going to have a real reporter in our class."

"A *real* reporter?" Brenda cried. She tossed a copy of the *Carlton News* at Nancy. "What am I—chopped liver?"

"Whoops," Nancy said as Brenda huffed off. "I forgot that Brenda is a reporter, too."

"Some reporter," George said. "What did Miss Snooty Pants write about today?"

Nancy held up the newspaper. The headline read, "Our School's Biggest Brats." Underneath were pictures of Jason Hutchings, David Berger, and Mike Minelli.

"You call that news?" George asked. "Everyone knows that the boys are the biggest brats in school."

"In the *world!*" Bess added.

The school bell rang.

George took the newspaper from Nancy. She dropped it in the recycle can. "So much for the *Carlton Pe-ews!*"

The girls walked into the school. They hurried through the hallway with the other students.

"I wore my favorite blouse and jumper just for Alice," Bess said. "In case she writes about our clothes."

George's dark curls bounced as she

4

shook her head. "Alice has more important things to write about than our clothes."

"Like what?" Bess asked.

George grinned. "Like Mrs. Carmichael's macaroni and cheese."

"Yum!" Nancy said.

Every Monday Mrs. Carmichael, the new lunch lady, made macaroni and cheese. It was so good that the girls never brought in their lunches on Mondays.

"There's Mrs. Carmichael now," Nancy said. "Let's ask her if she made chocolate pudding for dessert."

Mrs. Carmichael was standing right outside the lunchroom with Mr. Belsky, the music teacher. As the girls walked closer, Nancy could hear them talking.

"I hope Alice Stone likes my lunch," Mrs. Carmichael said. "I made chocolate pudding for dessert. With whipped cream."

"Ye-es!" George whispered.

"Were you really in the same third-grade class as Alice?" Mr. Belsky asked.

Nancy's eyes opened wide. She didn't

know that Mrs. Carmichael had gone to Carl Sandburg Elementary School, too.

"I sure was," Mrs. Carmichael replied. "Alice used to sit right in front of me. Her long ponytail kept getting stuck in my pencil case."

"Ouch!" Bess said. She grabbed her own ponytail. "That *has* to hurt!"

"Let's see if we can hear more about Alice," Nancy told her friends.

Nancy hurried over to the water fountain near Mrs. Carmichael. She listened closely as she began to drink.

"What was Alice like back then, Enid?" Mr. Belsky asked.

"Alice Stone was the bossiest girl in the third grade," Mrs. Carmichael said.

Nancy sputtered her water. Bossy?

"We even had a name for her," Mrs. Carmichael said. "Oh, yeah—we called her Miss Snobby Pants."

Nancy pulled herself away from the fountain. George began to drink.

"Miss Snobby Pants?" Nancy whispered. "Are you both thinking what I'm thinking?"

6

Bess nodded. "It sounds just like Brenda's nickname—Miss Snooty Pants."

A boy in the fourth grade tapped George's shoulder. "Are you going to leave me some water or what?" he asked.

George turned to the boy with puffed cheeks. She pretended to be about to spit.

"Come on," Nancy said, grabbing George's arm. "We'll be late for class."

"Do you think Alice Stone is anything like Brenda Carlton?" Bess asked as they walked through the hallway.

"Probably worse," George said. "Alice is a grown-up. That means she's had plenty of time to get even snootier."

"I hope Miss Snobby Pants doesn't sit next to me," Bess said as they walked into their classroom.

"Or me," George said.

Nancy didn't want Alice to sit next to her either. What would Miss Snobby Pants do? Copy her test paper? Throw spitballs? Make faces at her?

But when Nancy walked to her desk she froze. The seat next to hers was empty. The desk was completely cleared off.

"Good morning, class," Mrs. Reynolds said. She smiled at Nancy. "Guess what, Nancy? Alice Stone will be sitting right next to you!"

Next to me? Nancy thought. Her stomach did a double flip. Oh, no!

# 2

# Say Cheese!

That's not fair!" Brenda cried. "I invited Alice to our school. She should sit next to me!"

"The desk next to Nancy is empty this week, Brenda," Mrs. Reynolds said. "Orson Wong is absent with the flu."

"Then that desk is full of germs!" Brenda gasped. "Alice can't sit there!"

"Alice will be fine." Mrs. Reynolds smiled at Nancy. "And she'll like sitting next to the school's best detective."

Nancy smiled back. The whole class knew that she loved solving mysteries.

They even knew about her blue detective notebook. That's where Nancy wrote down all of her suspects and clues.

"Good morning!" a voice said.

Everyone turned around. A woman with dark hair stood by the door. She wore a pants suit and high-heeled shoes. She was carrying a big brown bag on her shoulder.

"I'm Alice Stone," the woman said. She handed Mrs. Reynolds a shiny apple. "And I'm ready for the third grade."

"How is she going to play tag in those shoes?" Bess whispered to Nancy.

"Welcome, Ms. Stone," Mrs. Reynolds said, taking the apple. "I mean, Alice."

Mrs. Reynolds showed Alice where to sit—right next to Nancy.

While Mrs. Reynolds wrote the date on the board, Alice turned to Nancy.

"Guess what I brought to school today?" Alice whispered.

"What?" Nancy whispered back.

Alice opened her bag just a bit. Inside

was a bright pink jump rope with silver sparkles on the handles.

"This was my lucky jump rope when I was in third grade," Alice said.

"It's awesome!" Nancy said with a smile. Alice didn't seem snobby at all!

Mrs. Reynolds took the roll. Then it was time to hand out the class jobs.

"David, Jason, and Mike," she said. "You'll wash the chalkboard during recess on Tuesday."

"And miss recess?" David complained.

"That's why I gave the job to all three of you," Mrs. Reynolds said. "So you can keep one another company."

Mrs. Reynolds turned to Alice. "I'm sure you had class jobs when you were in third grade," she said.

"I sure did," Alice said. "My favorite job was watering the plants."

"We have plants," Brenda cried out. "I'll bet Mrs. Reynolds will let you water the plants. Right, Mrs. Reynolds?"

"Emily Reeves is supposed to water the plants this week," Mrs. Reynolds said.

"But I'm sure she wouldn't mind giving Alice her job."

"What job would I have instead?" Emily asked. She looked worried.

Mrs. Reynolds glanced at her list. "I need someone to clean the hamster cage."

Nancy gasped. Cleaning the hamster cage was the yuckiest job in the class.

"The hamster cage?" Emily asked.

"Ha, ha," Jason snickered.

"Goody!" Brenda cried. "Now Alice gets her favorite job. Thanks to me!"

Nancy looked at Emily. She could tell she was very upset.

Mrs. Reynolds handed out more jobs. Nancy's job was to collect the quiz sheets. Bess would dust the bookshelf. George would empty the pencil sharpener.

When all the jobs had been given out, Andrew Leoni raised his hand. "Can I read a poem I wrote for Alice?" he asked.

"Sure, Andrew," Mrs. Reynolds said.

Andrew stood up with his notebook in his hands. He began to read:

*    *    *

"Welcome back to your old school.
 We hope your week with us is cool.
 And when you write about what you see,
 Don't forget to mention me!"

"Thanks, Andrew," Alice said. "You're a real poet."

"I am?" Andrew asked. "Cool!"

"Does anyone have a question for Alice about being a newspaper reporter?" Mrs. Reynolds asked the class.

Jason raised his hand. "Does Alice write the comic strips, too? *Oogie the Caveman* is my favorite."

Brenda whirled around in her seat. "Alice is a *serious* reporter, Jason," she said. "That was a dumb question!"

"What do you expect from one of the brattiest boys in school?" Jason sneered.

Nancy bit her lip. She knew that Jason was talking about Brenda's article.

"Settle down," Mrs. Reynolds said.

Nancy glanced at Alice. She was writing something in a small notepad—and she was smiling.

15

That's a good sign, Nancy thought. She must like our school so far.

After a social studies lesson and a math quiz it was time for lunch.

"Try the macaroni and cheese," Brenda told Alice on the lunch line. "And the chocolate pudding."

Nancy shook her head. Brenda was following Alice around like a puppy dog!

The girls pushed their trays down the line. Nancy could smell the hot macaroni and cheese. She couldn't wait to eat it.

"Morning is light, night is dark," Andrew called from the back of the line. "I'm so hungry I could eat a shark!"

"Give me a break," George complained. "Ever since Alice called Andrew a poet, he won't stop rhyming."

Mrs. Carmichael handed Alice a plate of macaroni and cheese. "I baked this just for you, Alice," she said.

"I usually have a salad," Alice said, taking the plate. "But this looks great!"

The girls carried their trays to a table.

Nancy was happy to see that Alice was sitting there, too. She wasn't so happy to see Brenda sitting next to her.

"I forgot a fork," Alice sighed. "Who wants to show me where they are?"

All four hands shot up.

"Why don't you *all* show me?" Alice asked. "The more the merrier."

"Someone has to stay here to watch our trays," Brenda said. She turned to Bess. "You do it, Bess."

"Why me?" Bess complained.

"Because you look very responsible, Bess," Alice said.

A proud smile spread across Bess's face. "No problem."

The girls showed Alice where Mrs. Carmichael kept the forks. They grabbed more napkins and returned to the table.

"Now I can finally try the best macaroni and cheese in the world," Alice said. She placed a napkin in her lap.

Nancy and her friends watched Alice put a heaping forkful into her mouth.

"Did you ever taste anything like it in your whole life, Alice?" Nancy asked.

Alice dropped her fork. Her lips puckered up like a raisin. "Mm-mmph!"

"What did you say?" George asked.

"Blaaaah!" Alice cried. "Yuck!"

Nancy stared at Alice. The reporter from *Today's Times* was turning green!

# 3

# Lunch—and a Hunch

**A**lice!" Nancy said. She patted the reporter on the back. "Are you all right?"

"My macaroni and cheese is s-s-sour!" Alice said. She took a big sip of juice.

Sour? Nancy carefully tasted her own lunch. "Mine tastes great," she said.

"Great?" Alice said. "It's the worst thing I ever tasted. Try it yourself."

Alice pushed her plate toward Nancy.

Nancy squeezed her eyes shut as she tasted Alice's macaroni and cheese.

"Ugh!" Nancy said. She wanted to spit it out. "It's sour, all right!"

"Like a lemon?" George asked.

Bess quickly tasted some, too. She shook her head. "Like Pucker Powder."

"Pucker Powder?" Brenda repeated.

"It's that candy that sprinkles like sugar but tastes sour," Bess said. "It's yummy. But not on macaroni and cheese."

"How come we couldn't see it on the macaroni and cheese?" Nancy asked.

"It must have been the pineapple flavor," Bess said. "It's light yellow."

"Someone sprinkled Pucker Powder on Alice's lunch?" Brenda turned to Bess. "I thought you were watching our trays."

"I was!" Bess cried. "I did!"

Brenda picked up Alice's plate. "I'm taking this back to Mrs. Carmichael."

"No, Brenda," Alice said. "I don't want to embarrass her."

"Then I'm throwing it right in the trash can!" Brenda declared.

"Sorry, Alice," Nancy said after Brenda left. "You can still get a tuna sandwich and chips."

Alice shook her head. "I'm not hungry anymore. Besides, I have some work to do."

Nancy watched as Alice took out her notepad. But this time as Alice wrote she wasn't smiling—she was frowning.

Uh-oh, Nancy thought. Bad news!

"Who would want to spoil Alice's lunch?" George asked later during recess. "She's so nice."

"Maybe someone who's not so nice," Nancy said with a shrug.

"Nancy, wait up!" a voice called.

"Speaking of not so nice," Bess whispered. "Here comes Brenda."

Brenda ran over and looked Nancy straight in the eye. "Alice can't write a bad article about our school," she said. "Not when the whole thing was my idea."

"Is that what you came over to tell us?" George asked.

Brenda shook her head. She pointed to Nancy. "I want Detective Drew to find out who poured Pucker Powder in Alice's

21

macaroni and cheese," she said. "Before the troublemaker strikes again!"

Nancy gave it a thought. The spoiled lunch *was* a mystery—and she loved solving mysteries.

"Well?" Brenda asked Nancy.

"Okay," Nancy said. "I'll do it."

George tapped Nancy's shoulder. "Um, Nancy? Can we talk? Just the three of us?"

Nancy, Bess, and George stepped away from Brenda.

"Why do you want to help Miss Snooty Pants, Nancy?" George whispered.

"Yeah," Bess said. "She's just going to get snootier and bossier."

"I'm not helping Brenda, I'm helping Alice," Nancy explained. "We all want her to write a good article about Carl Sandburg Elementary School, right?"

Bess and George nodded. Then they walked back to Brenda.

"I'll start this case right away, Brenda," Nancy said.

"Good. Because I'm going to check up

on you every day," Brenda declared. "To make sure you're doing your job."

"Check up on me?" Nancy gasped as Brenda strutted away.

"Come on, Nancy," George said, tugging her arm. "Just keep thinking about Alice and the article."

The girls sat down on a bench in the playground. Nancy pulled out her blue detective notebook. Bess and George looked over Nancy's shoulders as she opened her notebook to a clean page.

"I think I'll call this case Alice in Troubleland," Nancy said.

"I like that!" Bess giggled.

Nancy wrote the words on top of the page. On the next line she wrote "Trouble." Right under that she wrote "Pucker Powder."

"Now for my suspects," Nancy said. She wrote "Who?" on the next page. On the next line she wrote Emily's name.

"Why Emily?" George asked, surprised.

"Emily was mad that Alice got her job

23

and she has to clean the hamster cage," Nancy explained.

"I don't blame Emily," Bess said. She made a face. "That cage is gross!"

"But how could Emily ruin Alice's lunch?" George said. "Bess was watching our trays all the time. Right, Bess?"

"Sure," Bess said, nodding.

"Unless it was Mrs. Carmichael," Nancy said. "She handed Alice a plate of macaroni and cheese. And we heard her say that she once didn't like Alice."

"Hey! Maybe Mrs. Carmichael keeps Pucker Powder in her kitchen," Bess said. "Maybe we can search it."

George shook her head. "Mrs. Carmichael would never let us into her kitchen. It's a lost cause."

Lost? The word made Nancy jump.

"Bess, George!" Nancy said. "Mrs. Carmichael keeps a lost-and-found box in her kitchen. She lets the kids look inside it during recess, and it's recess now."

"Let's go for it!" George said.

The girls got permission from Mrs. Reynolds to go to the lunchroom. Once there they peeked through the kitchen door. Mrs. Carmichael was scrubbing the counters with a wet sponge.

"Hi, girls," Mrs. Carmichael said, looking up. "What can I do for you?"

"We'd like to look through your lost-and-found box, please," Nancy said.

"For what?" Mrs. Carmichael asked.

"Um," Nancy said.

"I lost my science project," George said quickly. "Can I look for it?"

"Sure," Mrs. Carmichael said. She narrowed her eyes. "As long as your science project doesn't have bugs."

Wow, Nancy thought. Mrs. Carmichael must really hate bugs.

"Nope," George said. "No bugs."

The girls walked through the kitchen door. Mrs. Carmichael held up her hand. "Stop! Right where you are!" she demanded.

Nancy, Bess, and George froze. Mrs. Carmichael pointed to a sign on the door: Do Not Enter Kitchen Without a Hair Net!

Mrs. Carmichael held out three white

hair nets. "It's what all fashionable lunch ladies are wearing this year," she joked.

"I can't wear that," Bess complained. "It'll mess up my butterfly clips."

George gave her cousin a nudge.

"Okay, okay," Bess said. She pulled the hair net over her head.

"Now you can come inside," Mrs. Carmichael said. The girls followed her into the kitchen.

"We can't search the kitchen with Mrs. Carmichael here," Nancy whispered.

George winked at Nancy. Then she turned to Mrs. Carmichael.

"Mrs. Carmichael?" she asked. "What does a water bug look like?"

"Water bug?" Mrs. Carmichael gasped. She began twisting the sponge. "Why?"

"Oh." George shrugged. "Because I think I just saw one in the lunchroom."

"A bug?" Mrs. Carmichael growled. She dropped her sponge. "Not in my lunchroom!"

Mrs. Carmichael grabbed a fly swatter and marched out of the kitchen.

"George?" Bess asked, worried. "You didn't really see a bug, did you?"

"No," George told Bess. She pushed up her sleeves. "Now, let's get to work."

Nancy ran to a white cabinet. She pulled the doors open and looked on the shelves. There were big cans of juice and bags of hot-dog buns, but no Pucker Powder. Then Nancy looked up. There was a big basket on the top shelf.

"Maybe it's up there," she said.

George dragged over a stool. She hopped on it and tugged at the basket.

"George!" Nancy whispered. "Be care—"

Crash! The basket toppled off the shelf. Hundreds of ketchup and mustard packets poured onto the floor.

"Whoops," George mumbled.

Nancy's heart was pounding. "Quick!" she said. "Let's put these back!"

But as the girls stepped on top of the packets, they burst open, squirting ketchup and mustard all over the floor!

"Yuck!" Bess cried. "It's all over my new sneakers!"

"What is going on in here?" a voice demanded.

Nancy dropped a handful of ketchup packets. The voice belonged to Mrs. Carmichael.

They were in big trouble!

# 4

# Trouble Strikes Again

**D**id you find the bug, Mrs. Carmichael?" Bess asked in a small voice.

Mrs. Carmichael folded her arms across her chest. "Look at this mess. Ketchup and mustard all over the floor!"

"Where are hot dogs when you need them?" George asked with a nervous laugh.

"Sorry, Mrs. Carmichael," Nancy said. "We were looking for Pucker Powder."

"Pucker what?" Mrs. Carmichael asked.

Nancy took a deep breath. She told Mrs. Carmichael everything about Alice and the macaroni and cheese.

"No one messes up my lunch and gets away with it!" Mrs. Carmichael growled.

Nancy nodded. "That's why we were trying to find out who the troublemaker was, Mrs. Carmichael."

Mrs. Carmichael raised an eyebrow. "And you thought it was me?" she asked.

"We heard you say that you didn't like Alice in the third grade," Bess said

"That was back in third grade," Mrs. Carmichael said. "Now we're good friends."

"Friends?" Nancy asked.

"You bet!" Mrs. Carmichael said. "In fact, I'll tell you girls a secret."

The girls leaned forward.

"Alice is helping me write my first cookbook," Mrs. Carmichael said. It's called 'The Joy of School Lunches.'"

"Wow!" George said. "Will it have your recipe for macaroni and cheese?"

Mrs. Carmichael nodded. "There's even a whole chapter on fried fish sticks."

Nancy, Bess, and George helped Mrs. Carmichael pick up the ketchup and mustard packets. They thanked Mrs. Carmichael and left the kitchen.

"I'll cross Mrs. Carmichael's name out of my notebook after school," Nancy said as they walked through the hall.

"I don't get it," George said. "Mrs. Carmichael handed Alice her plate. And Bess was watching our trays when we walked away. Right, Bess?"

"Right," Bess said. She shrugged. "At least most of the time."

Nancy and George stopped walking.

"*Most* of the time?" Nancy asked.

"You left the table?" George cried.

"Just for a minute," Bess said. "Molly Angelo was passing out her mom's home-baked cookies at the next table. I had to get one. Or two. Or maybe I had three."

"You were supposed to watch our macaroni and cheese, Bess," George said.

"I did watch it!" Bess cried. "Right after I got the cookies."

"It's okay, Bess," Nancy said. "At least now we know the culprit could have been anyone in the lunchroom."

The girls hurried through the hall to

their classroom. Mrs. Carmichael had given them a special late pass.

Nancy opened the door. When they stepped inside everyone was reading from their science books. One by one they looked up and began to laugh.

"What's so funny?" Nancy whispered.

"Bears are brown, elephants are gray," Andrew called out. "Someone's having . . . a bad hair day!"

Bess grabbed her head. "Oh, no. We forgot to take off our hair nets!"

Nancy felt her cheeks burn.

The things I do to solve a case, Nancy thought. Amazing!

"Is Mrs. Carmichael's macaroni and cheese better than mine?" Hannah Gruen asked Nancy at dinner.

Hannah had been the Drews' housekeeper since Nancy was three years old. That's when Nancy's mother died.

Nancy wrapped her arms around Hannah's waist and gave her a hug. "I love your macaroni and cheese, Hannah."

"Good," Hannah said. She placed a

bowl of rolls on the table. "But today we're having meatloaf."

"Without Pucker Powder, I hope," Mr. Drew joked. He reached over and ruffled Nancy's reddish blond bangs.

Nancy smiled. She had just told her dad about Alice and the macaroni and cheese. Mr. Drew was a lawyer and liked to help Nancy with her cases.

"Now I have only one suspect, Daddy," Nancy sighed. "And that's Emily."

"Is there anyone else who might be mad at Alice?" Mr. Drew asked.

Nancy grabbed a roll and shrugged. "If there is, I don't have a clue."

Hannah poured Nancy a glass of milk. "It could just be a troublemaker," she said. "Someone who's up to no good."

"Troublemaker?" Nancy repeated. She dropped the roll on her plate. "Or three!"

"What do you mean, Pudding Pie?" Mr. Drew asked.

"Jason, David, and Mike!" Nancy said excitedly. "They're always up to no good."

"Remember, Nancy," Mr. Drew said, "before you accuse anyone, there's one thing a detective always needs."

"I know," Nancy said. "Proof!"

Nancy smiled and took a sip of milk.

I may not have proof yet, she thought. But I do have three more suspects. And that's a great start!

"The boys!" George said the next morning as they entered their classroom. "Why didn't I think of them?"

"It wasn't hard to figure out," Nancy said. "Everyone knows the boys are brats."

"Yeah. And they probably like Pucker Powder, too," George said.

Bess looked hurt. "I like Pucker Powder and I'm not a brat."

Nancy hung up her jacket. She sat down at her desk next to Alice.

"I brought my lunch to school today, Nancy," Alice said. She held up a small brown paper bag. "No more macaroni and cheese for me."

A note fell on Nancy's desk. Nancy

looked up and saw Brenda walking away.

Nancy unfolded the note. It read: "Did you find the troublemaker yet????"

Nancy wrote a big "no" on the note. She passed it back to Brenda and watched her read it.

Brenda shook her head. She crumpled the note and tossed it on the floor!

Nancy quickly wrote Brenda another note. This time it read: "Pick it up! You shouldn't litter!"

The morning went fast for Nancy. Soon it was time for lunch and then recess.

Nancy, Bess, and George discussed the case on the swings in the playground.

"No trouble so far," Nancy said. "And it's already the middle of the day."

"Maybe the troublemaker gave up." Bess said. She crossed her fingers hard.

Nancy was about to swing higher when she heard Alice cry out: "Oh, no!"

Nancy stopped swinging and turned around. Alice was near the seesaws. She

37

looked worried as she dug through her bag.

"My lucky jump rope!" Alice cried. "It's gone!"

"Gone?" Nancy jumped off the swing. "No way!"

# 5

# Backpack Attack

I know I packed the jump rope this morning," Alice said as the girls ran over. "It was in my bag during lunch when I reached for my notepad."

"Did you put your bag down during recess?" Nancy asked. "At all?"

"Only when I went on the seesaw," Alice said sadly. "And now the jump rope is missing."

"Don't worry, Alice," Bess said. "Nancy is a detective. She'll help you find your jump rope."

The girls and Alice searched the playground. They even asked other kids if they'd seen it. No luck.

"Do you want us to tell Mrs. Reynolds?" Nancy asked Alice.

"No," Alice said seriously. "I'll take care of this in my own way."

"What do you mean?" Nancy asked.

Alice pulled her notepad out of her bag. "By writing about it," she said.

"Oh, great," George whispered. "More bad news about our school."

Nancy had something to write, too. She took out her notebook and opened it to her Trouble list. Under "Macaroni and Cheese" she wrote "Missing Jump Rope."

Now two horrible things have happened to Alice, Nancy thought. And that's two too many!

"I can give Alice my old jump rope," George said after school. "If she doesn't mind bubblegum on the handles."

"George!" Bess cried. "That's gross!"

"I don't think Alice wants another jump rope," Nancy told George. "Her old jump rope was special. She'd had it since she was eight years old."

The girls began walking home. When they were a block away from the school Nancy felt someone bump into her shoulder.

"Excuse us!" Jason's voice growled.

Jason, David, and Mike pushed their way past the girls.

"You shouldn't push!" Nancy yelled.

"I said, excuse me!" Jason growled.

Nancy's eyes fell on Jason's backpack. Stuffed inside the back pocket was something long and skinny—something that looked like a jump rope!

"Bess! George!" Nancy said in a low voice. "Check out Jason's backpack."

"Is that the jump rope?" Bess gasped.

"There's only one way to find out," Nancy said. She narrowed her eyes. "Let's question him."

"Freeze!" George yelled to the boys.

"Like an icicle!" Bess shouted.

The boys stopped. They turned around and folded their arms.

"What do you want?" Jason asked.

"I want to know what's inside your backpack pocket," Nancy said.

"Alice's jump rope was stolen during recess," George said. "Did you take it?"

A sly smile spread over Jason's face. "Maybe I did. Maybe I didn't."

"I bet that means yes," Bess said.

The three boys snickered. They turned around and raced up the block.

"Get them!" George yelled.

Nancy panted as they chased the boys. It wasn't easy running with schoolbooks. But George was a fast runner and caught up to the boys.

"Gotcha!" George shouted. She grabbed onto Jason's backpack.

"Get off me!" Jason yelled. His backpack fell to the ground. "Now look what you made me do!"

George didn't answer. She reached into the back pocket. But when she pulled out her hand she wasn't holding a jump rope. She was holding a green-and-brown, slimy—

"Snake!" George yelled.

The girls screamed as they tossed the

wiggly snake back and forth. But the boys were laughing their heads off.

"Scaredy-cats! Scaredy-cats!" Jason sneered. "Scared of a fake snake!"

Fake snake? Nancy dropped the snake. It lay on the ground without a wiggle.

"It looked real to me," George said.

Nancy looked at the boys. "You still could have stolen the jump rope."

"How could we?" David sneered. "We didn't even have recess today."

"Huh?" George said.

"It's Tuesday," Jason said. "It was our day to wash the chalkboard. Remember?"

"And if you don't believe us," Mike said, "you can ask Mrs. Reynolds."

Nancy had completely forgotten about the boys' Tuesday job.

"We believe you," Nancy sighed.

"But we don't *like* you," Bess said.


"Slow down, Chocolate Chip!" Nancy told her chocolate Labrador puppy later that afternoon. She gave Chip's leash a tug.

44

"She's getting big," Bess said. "Soon you'll have to call her Chocolate Cookie."

Nancy smiled. "Thanks for walking her with me, you guys."

"It's fun," George said. "And while we walk Chip we can talk about the case."

"Some case," Nancy sighed. "I just crossed the boys out of my notebook. Now Emily is my only suspect again."

The girls walked Chip three blocks away from Nancy's house.

"Hey!" Bess said. She stopped walking and looked around. "This is the block where Emily lives. I know it is!"

"How do you know?" Nancy asked.

"In second grade she invited me over for milk and caramel fudge cookies," Bess said. "But I don't remember which house she lives in."

"You remember the cookies but not the house?" George said.

Bess shrugged. "They were yummy."

The girls walked Chip up the block. Suddenly George grabbed Nancy's arm. "There's Emily!" she whispered.

Nancy looked to see where George was

pointing. She saw Emily jumping rope in front of a light blue house.

All of a sudden she saw something else. Emily's jump rope was bright pink with sparkly handles!

"Ohmygosh," Nancy gasped. "Alice's jump rope!"

# 6

# Alice, Go Home!

"Teddy bear, teddy bear, turn around," Emily sang as she jumped rope.

"Nancy?" George whispered. "Is that the same jump rope Alice showed you?"

"Maybe," Nancy whispered back. "But I don't want to jump to any conclusions."

"Jump!" Bess laughed. "Like the jump rope. That's funny, Nancy!"

"Shh," Nancy said. "I don't want Emily to know we're watching her."

Nancy pulled Chip behind a tree near Emily's yard. Bess and George followed.

It sure looks like Alice's jump rope, Nancy thought as she peeked out.

Just then a squirrel scurried down from the tree. Chip barked and pulled as the squirrel ran into Emily's yard.

"Chip, wait!" Nancy cried. She tried to hold the puppy back. Bess and George grabbed the leash, too. But it was no use. Chip was pulling with all her might.

Emily stared as all three girls stumbled after Chip into her yard.

"Hi," Emily said.

The squirrel disappeared between a row of bushes. Chip whined.

"Hi, Emily," Nancy said. "We were just walking my dog."

"It looked like she was walking *you*." Emily giggled.

Nancy decided to get right to the point. "Is that a brand-new jump rope, Emily?" she asked.

Emily's eyes opened wide. She looked scared. "No!" she said quickly. "I mean— yes! I mean—I have to feed my fish!"

Emily turned around and ran into the house.

"Emily didn't have fish," Bess said slowly. "That I remember, too."

"Speaking of fishy—did you see her face?" George asked. "She's guilty."

"I don't want to accuse Emily until I speak to her tomorrow in school," Nancy said. She looked at her watch. "I'd better take Chip home now, before it gets late."

"Or before another squirrel shows up!" Bess giggled.

Nancy smiled as she walked Chip home. The pink jump rope with the sparkly handles was her best clue yet. She couldn't wait to write it in her notebook.

"What do you want on your spinach salad, Nancy?" Hannah asked before dinner. She was cutting mushrooms on the counter.

Nancy looked up from the napkins she was folding. "Butterscotch chips and rainbow sprinkles," she said.

"Very funny!" Hannah said with a smile. The phone rang. Hannah answered it.

"Drew residence. Yes, she is," Hannah said. She held the receiver out to Nancy. "It's for you. It's Brenda."

"Great," Nancy mumbled. She took the receiver. "Hi, Brenda."

"Well? Did you find the troublemaker yet?" Brenda asked in a hurried voice.

"Not yet," Nancy said. "But I think I'm getting close."

"Not good enough," Brenda snapped. "A photographer from *Today's Times* is coming to school tomorrow. Nothing can go wrong!"

"I said I was close," Nancy said. "And I'm working as hard as I can."

"Well, work harder," Brenda said. "Because if Alice writes a crummy article about our school, it will be *your* fault!"

Nancy heard a click.

"Toast," Nancy mumbled as she hung up the phone.

"You want toast with your dinner?" Hannah asked, surprised.

"No, Hannah," Nancy said. "That's what I'll be if I don't solve this case soon—toast!"

\* \* \*

"Brenda-ish!" George said the next morning. "Miss Snooty Pants was just being Brenda-ish again."

Nancy had just told Bess and George about Brenda's nasty phone call.

"Were you upset, Nancy?" Bess asked.

"Sort of," Nancy said. "After she called I couldn't eat my spinach salad."

"That's okay," Bess said, making a face. "I can *never* eat that stuff."

The girls hung up their jackets. Nancy looked around the classroom. A man was taking pictures of Alice watering the plants. He wore a baseball cap with the name Luke stitched onto it.

I'll bet that's the photographer from *Today's Times*, Nancy thought.

She saw Emily kneeling by the hamster cage and scrubbing the bars with a cloth.

"Let's ask Emily about the jump rope," Nancy told Bess and George.

Nancy could hear Emily muttering as they stepped behind her.

"I hate this job. Hate it. Hate it."

"Hi, Emily," Nancy said.

Emily looked over her shoulder. "Oh, hi, Nancy." She sighed.

"Is the hamster cage really messy this week?" Bess asked.

"Totally gross," Emily said. She scowled at Alice. "If it weren't for Alice, I'd be watering the plants."

"She's our special guest," Nancy reminded Emily. "And speaking of Alice, your jump rope looked exactly like hers."

"Her *stolen* jump rope," Bess added.

Emily's mouth dropped open. "You mean it was Alice's jump rope? I didn't know."

"Then how did you get it?" George asked.

Emily stood up and whispered, "Someone in our class gave it to me."

"Who?" Nancy asked.

Emily shook her head. "My lips are zipped. I promised I wouldn't tell."

Nancy was disappointed. But Emily was right—a promise was a promise.

"Okay, Emily," Nancy said. "But can you promise *me* something?"

"What?" Emily asked.

"That you'll give Alice her jump rope first thing tomorrow?" Nancy said.

"Sure," Emily nodded. "I had no idea that it belonged to her."

After everyone was seated Mrs. Reynolds called for attention.

"We're going to be famous," Mrs. Reynolds said. "Luke would like to take a picture of us for *Today's Times*."

Everyone whispered excitedly.

"How about a picture in the school yard?" Brenda suggested.

"Great idea, Brenda!" Luke said.

Everyone lined up. Mrs. Reynolds led the class outside to the school yard.

While Luke loaded film into his camera, Nancy, Bess, and George waited by Alice's welcome sign.

"Emily didn't steal the jump rope," Nancy said. She crossed Emily's name out of her notebook.

"Then who did?" Bess asked.

Nancy looked around the school yard at her classmates. "It could be anyone."

"Poor Alice," George said. She looked up at Alice's third-grade picture. "I wonder if she had this much trouble when she was in third grade."

"Okay, kids!" Luke called. "Let's gather around for a group shot!"

Nancy quickly slipped her notebook into her jacket pocket.

"I know, I know," Brenda said. "How about a picture in front of the flagpole?"

"Fabulous idea, Brenda!" Luke said. "What would we do without you?"

Nancy rolled her eyes. Luke was just being nice to Brenda because her father owned *Today's Times*.

Luke set up his camera on a stand with three long legs.

Mrs. Reynolds waved to Kyle Leddington, who was on the swings. "Kyle, this isn't recess. Come join us now."

"Coming," Kyle said, still swinging.

"I want to stand next to Alice!" Phoebe Archer said, jumping up and down.

"Me, too!" Mari Cheng said.

"Mrs. Reynolds," Jenny Marsh complained, "I heard Peter say he was going to make a face in the picture."

"Did not!" Peter DeSands argued.

Mrs. Reynolds began to count the students. "One . . . two . . . three . . ."

"There's no time for that," Luke said. "I have lots of pictures to take."

Mrs. Reynolds nodded. She turned to the students. "Face the camera, boys and girls," she said. "Quickly now."

Some kids bumped into one another as they gathered in front of the flagpole. Nancy stood between Bess and George.

"Wait for meeeee!" Kyle yelled as he ran over from the swings.

Mrs. Reynolds looked angry. "Kyle," she said. "I told you to—"

"Say cheese!" Luke interrupted.

"Pepperoni!" Andrew yelled.

Nancy smiled one of her biggest smiles. Then she heard a click. The picture was taken.

"Where should we pose next?" Luke asked, looking up from the camera.

"On the moon!" Jason joked.

Nancy saw Jason, David, and Mike chasing one another around the flagpole.

"I know," Brenda said. "How about in front of Alice's welcome sign?"

Alice waved her hand. "Last one there is a rotten egg!" she called out.

Nancy and her classmates raced to the welcome sign. As they got closer, everyone froze one by one.

"Nancy, look!" Bess said slowly.

Nancy's jaw dropped as she stared at the sign. Someone had crossed out the word "Welcome" and written, "Go Home!"

Alice's third-grade picture was messed up, too. All of her teeth except one were filled in with a black marker!

"Oh, great," Nancy groaned. She stared at the picture and the welcome sign. "Some welcome!"

# 7

# Picture Perfect

"Cold in winter, hot in summer," Andrew rhymed. "This is really a major bummer."

"Shut up with your stupid poems!" Brenda yelled at Andrew. She reached out and touched the sign. "This is horrible!"

"Did anyone in our class do this?" Mrs. Reynolds asked angrily.

No one said a word.

"It couldn't have been someone in this class, Mrs. Reynolds," Alice said. "We were all posing for the picture."

Nancy glanced at her classmates. Everyone seemed to be there.

"I'd like to believe that, Alice," Mrs. Reynolds said. "But if anyone in our class did this, I'd like that student to come forward and apologize."

Silence.

"All right, then," Mrs. Reynolds said. "Let's go back to our classroom."

Nancy was about to line up when Brenda grabbed her arm.

"Ow!" Nancy complained.

"That was the last straw!" Brenda hissed. "I'm a reporter, too, you know!"

"So?" Nancy asked.

"So I'm going to write my *own* article for the *Carlton News*," Brenda said. "About what a bad detective Nancy Drew is!"

Bad detective? The words hit Nancy like a ton of bricks. Everyone thought she was the *best* detective in school. A bad article about her would spoil everything.

For the next few hours Nancy couldn't think of anything but Brenda's threat.

When it was time for lunch Nancy unwrapped her turkey sandwich. Then she discussed everything with Bess and George.

"The poster was fine at first," Nancy said. "The troublemaker must have struck while we were taking the picture."

"But we all posed for the picture," George said. "Just the way Alice said."

"Someone could have sneaked off," Nancy said. "But how can we know who?"

Nancy glanced around the lunchroom. Phoebe and Molly were sitting in the middle of her table. Alice was sitting at the other end next to Brenda. Luke was taking Alice's picture again.

"Okay, Alice!" Luke was saying. He twisted the lens on his camera. "Look up from your sandwich and say cheese."

"But it's tuna!" Alice joked.

Brenda laughed loudly. "Tuna! That is *so* funny, Alice," she said.

Nancy watched Luke snap the picture. An idea flashed inside her head.

"Wait a minute," Nancy said slowly. "If we look at the group picture we can see if anyone was missing."

"Yeah!" George cried.

"Let's ask Luke," Bess said.

The girls ran over to Luke. He was taking a picture of a colorful food mural.

"Luke? Can we look at the picture you took by the flagpole?" Nancy asked.

Luke shook his head. "That picture isn't ready yet. I'm developing it early tomorrow morning."

Tomorrow? Nancy thought. Tomorrow is Thursday—Alice's last day!

"Can we watch?" Nancy asked. "It's real important."

"No one is allowed inside *Today's Times*," Luke said. "Unless you know someone who works there."

"Oh," Nancy said, disappointed.

"Don't worry, girls," Luke said. "I'm sure you all came out great."

Nancy, Bess, and George trudged back to their table.

"They'd let Brenda inside *Today's Times*," George complained. "Her father owns the whole newspaper."

Nancy grabbed George's arm. "Brenda—

of course! Maybe *she* can get us into *Today's Times*."

Nancy found Brenda on the lunch line, looking at desserts.

"Hi, Brenda," Nancy said. "The cherry pie is awesome."

"I hate cherries," Brenda snapped. "What do you want anyway?"

"Can your dad take us to *Today's Times* tomorrow morning?" Nancy asked.

"You mean as a class trip?" Brenda asked.

"Not exactly," Nancy said.

"Then why do you want to go?" Brenda asked. She looked annoyed.

"Because—"

"Because we think Jason put donkey ears behind your head," George said quickly.

"What?" Brenda gasped.

"He put two fingers behind your head like this," George said. She stuck two fingers up behind Bess's head. "Hee-haw! Hee-haw! Hee-haw!"

"Quit it," Bess said, giggling.

Brenda looked around the lunchroom.

"When I find Jason I'll turn him inside out!" she said angrily.

"Wait, Brenda," Nancy said. "Luke is developing the picture early tomorrow morning. Why don't you look at it first? To make sure it's true."

Brenda's face was red as she thought about it. Then she nodded.

"I'll ask my dad to take me tomorrow morning," Brenda said. "He can drive me to school after I look at the picture."

"Us, too?" Nancy asked hopefully.

"Only if you're at my house at seven-thirty in the morning," Brenda said. "That's when my father leaves for work."

"But I eat my Tooty Fruity Flakes at seven-thirty," Bess complained.

"We'll be there," George promised.

Nancy gave her friends a thumbs-up sign behind her back. The plan had worked.

"Here it is, girls," Mr. Carlton said early Thursday morning. *Today's Times!*

"Wow!" Nancy said. She looked around the newspaper office. It was filled with people sitting at desks and working on computers. Others were rushing around.

"The reporters get some of the news on their computers," Mr. Carlton explained.

A man wearing glasses ran over. "There's a broken water pipe on Beech Street, Mr. Carlton," he said.

"A water pipe?" Mr. Carlton said. He frowned at the man. "Leonard, I want that story on my desk in an hour!"

"Yes, sir," Leonard said. He bumped into others as he ran to his desk.

Mr. Carlton put his arm around Brenda's shoulders. "Someday you'll own *Today's Times,* Cupcake," he said.

"Yes, Daddy," Brenda said. "But then it will be called *Brenda's Times.*"

"I think I'm going to barf," George whispered to Nancy.

Luke walked over. He was carrying a cup of coffee and a donut.

"Luke," Mr. Carlton said. "The girls are here to see one of your pictures. Why don't you show them the darkroom?"

"Darkroom?" Bess squeaked. "But I'm afraid of the dark. Sometimes."

"The darkroom is where we develop the film," Luke explained. "It's not totally dark."

The girls followed Luke to a door in the back of the office. A sign over it read: Do Not Enter When Red Light Is On.

"This is it," Luke said, opening the door. The girls stepped inside the room. It was lit with a soft red light.

Nancy looked around the darkroom. There were all kinds of strange machines and a counter covered with metal pans. Black-and-white pictures were hanging on a string with clothespins.

"Why are those pictures wet?" Nancy asked.

"We use a special liquid to develop the film," Luke said. "It's called—"

"We don't have time for a tour!" Brenda snapped. "Where's the group picture?"

Luke picked up a piece of white paper. "I've already enlarged the negative," he said. "Now I'll develop it."

Luke placed the paper in a pan of liquid. He swished the paper around. Slowly, a picture began to appear on the paper. It was the group picture in front of the flagpole.

"It's like magic!" Bess gasped.

Nancy counted her classmates. "Molly, Jenny, Andrew," she whispered. "Mari—"

"Oh, good." Brenda sighed with relief. "No donkey ears."

"Kyle, Phoebe, Peter—"

"In fact," Brenda went on, "the boys aren't even *in* the picture."

Nancy looked up. "The boys?"

Nancy, Bess, and George shoved Brenda aside as they leaned over the pan.

"Hey!" Brenda complained.

"Look!" Nancy said. She pointed to the picture. "The boys *are* missing!"

# 8

# Gotcha!

**B**ut you crossed the boys out of your notebook, Nancy," Bess said.

"I know," Nancy said. "But now I have new evidence. *Great* evidence!"

"What are you talking about?" Brenda cried. "Are you keeping a secret from me?"

"We wanted to see if anyone was missing from the group picture," Nancy told Brenda. "Then we would know who might have messed up Alice's welcome sign."

Brenda put her hands on her hips. "I thought we were here to see if the boys put donkey ears behind my head."

"This is more important, Brenda,"

Nancy said. "We might have found the troublemakers."

Brenda dropped her hands. "That *is* important."

Nancy turned to Luke. "May we borrow the picture to show to Mrs. Reynolds?"

"Absolutely not," Luke said. "This picture belongs to *Today's Times*."

"We need it!" Brenda interrupted. "Give it to us now."

"Sure, Brenda," Luke said.

They waited a few minutes for the picture to dry. Then Mr. Carlton drove the girls to school. They ran into the classroom just as the bell rang.

"Mrs. Reynolds!" Brenda called. "Nancy has something to show you!"

Nancy pulled the picture out of a brown envelope.

"Everyone is in the group picture except for Jason, David, and Mike," Nancy said. "That means they might have been over by Alice's welcome sign."

"That's a lie!" Jason called out.

"Mrs. Reynolds!" a girl's voice screamed. "Mrs. Reynolds—look!"

Everyone turned around. Nancy saw Emily standing behind her desk. She was holding something between two fingers. It was the green-and-brown rubber snake.

"Look what was in my desk," Emily cried, her voice shaking. "Yuck!"

"That's the same rubber snake that was in Jason's backpack," George said.

"Jason?" Mrs. Reynolds asked. "Did you put that snake in Emily's desk?"

"No!" Jason cried. "It was supposed to be in *Alice's* desk. I mean—I mean—"

David slapped his forehead with his hand. "Busted," he groaned.

"In my desk?" Alice asked.

Emily dug into her backpack. She pulled out the pink jump rope with the sparkly handles. "The boys also gave me this," she said angrily. "And they made me promise I wouldn't tell!"

"My jump rope!" Alice cried.

Mrs. Reynolds put her hands on her hips. "I think Jason, David, and Mike have some explaining to do," she said.

Mike took a deep breath. "Okay, okay. We took Alice's jump rope before recess."

"Why did you give it to *me?*" Emily demanded.

"We wanted to get rid of the evidence," Jason said.

"And we didn't want to get caught with a girl's jump rope," David said.

Nancy glared at the boys. "Did you also pour Pucker Powder on Alice's macaroni and cheese?" she asked.

"How did you know?" David asked. He looked surprised.

"Does that mean yes?" Nancy asked.

"Okay, we did that, too," Jason admitted. "But you still don't have proof that we messed up the welcome sign."

"Yeah!" Mike said.

Nancy looked at the picture. She could see the school in the background. She could also see three tiny figures standing at the door. But who were they?

Nancy snapped her fingers. She ran to the science shelf and grabbed the magnifying glass. She placed it over the tiny

figures. Through the glass she could see Jason, David, and Mike.

"Proof!" Nancy said with a smile.

Mrs. Reynolds peered through the magnifying glass. Then she looked up and frowned at the boys.

"I just want to know one thing," Mrs. Reynolds said. "Why did you cause so much trouble for Alice? Don't you like her?"

"Sure, we do," Jason said.

"We wanted to get Brenda's goat by spoiling Alice's article," David said.

"She called us the school's biggest brats," Mike said. "So I guess we wanted to get even."

"You little creeps!" Brenda cried.

Mrs. Reynolds held up her hands for attention. "Now it's *my* turn to get even," she said. "You boys are going to write letters of apology to Alice. Then you're going to have a special class job for the rest of the school year."

"What?" David asked slowly.

"You're all going to clean the hamster cage," Mrs. Reynolds said sternly.

Everyone laughed except for the boys. Nancy could see that they looked sick.

"Well, Nancy," Alice said. "You really are a good detective."

"Thanks, Alice," Nancy said. She looked over at Brenda. Miss Snooty Pants was actually smiling at her. It was only a half smile from one side of her mouth, but it was still a smile. Amazing!

"Roses are red, violets are blue," Andrew rhymed. "Another case solved by Detective Drew."

"Yay, Nancy!" Bess cheered.

As they walked to the coat closet, Nancy turned to Alice. "Are you still going to write a bad article about our school?" she asked.

"I was never going to write a bad article," Alice admitted.

"You weren't?" Bess asked.

"I had a great time here this week," Alice said. "In fact, Jason, David, and Mike remind me of two boys who used to be in my class. Their names were Victor and Joel. They were always making trouble!"

"Does that mean our school is exactly as you remember it?" George asked.

"Exactly!" Alice said with a smile.

Nancy hung up her jacket. Then she sat down at her desk, opened her detective notebook and began to write:

Good news! Now everyone will know what a great school Carl Sandburg Elementary really is. I also learned something important in this case: if Miss Snobby Pants can grow up to be someone as nice as Alice—then maybe there's hope for Brenda Carlton!

Case closed.

# EASY TO READ—FUN TO SOLVE!

## Meet up with suspense and mystery in The Hardy Boys® are:

# THE CLUES™ BROTHERS

Available from Minstrel® Books
Published by Pocket Books